Dear Parent:

Congratulations! Your child is taking the first steps on an exciting journey. The destination? Independent reading!

STEP INTO READING® will help your child get there. The program offers five steps to reading success. Each step includes fun stories and colorful art. There are also Step into Reading Sticker Books, Step into Reading Math Readers, Step into Reading Write-In Readers, Step into Reading Phonics Readers, and Step into Reading Phonics First Steps! Boxed Sets—a complete literacy program with something for every child.

Learning to Read, Step by Step!

Ready to Read   Preschool–Kindergarten
• big type and easy words • rhyme and rhythm • picture clues
For children who know the alphabet and are eager to begin reading.

Reading with Help   Preschool–Grade 1
• basic vocabulary • short sentences • simple stories
For children who recognize familiar words and sound out new words with help.

Reading on Your Own   Grades 1–3
• engaging characters • easy-to-follow plots • popular topics
For children who are ready to read on their own.

Reading Paragraphs   Grades 2–3
• challenging vocabulary • short paragraphs • exciting stories
For newly independent readers who read simple sentences with confidence.

Ready for Chapters   Grades 2–4
• chapters • longer paragraphs • full-color art
For children who want to take the plunge into chapter books but still like colorful pictures.

STEP INTO READING® is designed to give every child a successful reading experience. The grade levels are only guides. Children can progress through the steps at their own speed, developing confidence in their reading, no matter what their grade.

Remember, a lifetime love of reading starts with a single step!

For Bobby and Riley
—C.G.

To lovely Elsie
—J.W.

Text copyright © 2008 by Charles Ghigna
Illustrations copyright © 2008 by Julia Woolf

Step into Reading, Random House, and the Random House colophon are registered trademarks of Random House, Inc.

Visit us on the Web! www.stepintoreading.com

Educators and librarians, for a variety of teaching tools, visit us at www.randomhouse.com/teachers

ISBN 978-0-375-87133-7

Printed in the United States of America

10 9 8 7 6 5 4 3 2 1

STEP INTO READING®

STEP 2

Snow Wonder

by Charles Ghigna

illustrated by Julia Woolf

Random House 🏠 New York

We wake and wonder
at the snow.
It puts on
such a lovely show.

The snowflakes
dance before our eyes.
Each snowflake
is a different size.

We grab our hats
and boots and coats.
We run outside
to play.

The snow has turned
the world all white and
made a brand-new day.

7

It's no wonder
that we cheer
snowflakes
when they fall each year.

It's no wonder
that we slide
sleds across
the countryside.

A chilly wind
comes rushing in.
We zip our coats
up to our chins.

Grandma calls.

It's time to go.

We hurry in

from the snow.

Baking cookies
in the kitchen,
we help Grandma
roll the dough.

Cookie cutter.

Lots of clutter.

Gingerbread men

in a row.

We drink cocoa
by the fire.
Grandpa reads
our favorite book.

The snow outside
is getting deeper.
We all run
to take a look.

It's no wonder
snowmen grow
from our garden
made of snow.

It's no wonder
that we skate
across the lake
a figure eight.

It's no wonder
that we roam
a moonlit path
back to our home.

It's *snow* wonder
that we sleep
snuggled warm
in blankets deep.